Luke Goes to Bat

RACHEL
ISADORA

G. P. Putnam's Sons
New York

P9-BZF-261

For Nicholas "39"

The game in this story is based on an actual one that took place
in Philadelphia between the Dodgers and the Phillies in 1951.
In the fourteenth inning, after a ball and a strike, Jackie Robinson
hit a home run that won the game, 9–8, for the Dodgers.

Copyright © 2005 by Rachel Isadora.

All rights reserved. This book, or parts thereof, may not be
reproduced in any form without permission in writing from the
publisher, G. P. Putnam's Sons, a division of Penguin Young Readers
Group, 345 Hudson Street, New York, NY 10014. G. P. Putnam's
Sons, Reg. U.S. Pat. & Tm. Off. The scanning, uploading and
distribution of this book via the Internet or via any other means
without the permission of the publisher is illegal and punishable by
law. Please purchase only authorized electronic editions, and do not
participate in or encourage electronic piracy of copyrighted materials.
Your support of the author's rights is appreciated.

Published simultaneously in Canada.
Manufactured in China by South China Printing Co. Ltd.
Designed by Cecilia Yung and Gunta Alexander. Text set in Administer.
The art was done in (tk).
Library of Congress Cataloging-in-Publication Data
Isadora, Rachel. Luke goes to bat / Rachel Isadora. p. cm.
Summary: Luke is not very good at baseball, but his grandmother and
sports star Jackie Robinson encourage him to keep trying.
[1. Baseball—Fiction. 2. Perseverance (Ethics)—Fiction. 3. Robinson,
Jackie, 1919–1972—Fiction. 4. Grandmothers—Fiction.] I. Title.
PZ7.I763Luk 2005 [E]—dc22 2004001890 ISBN 0-399-23604-X
10 9 8 7 6 5
Special Markets ISBN 978-0-399-24669-2
Not for Resale

This Imagination Library edition is published by Penguin Group (USA), a Pearson
company, exclusively for Dolly Parton's Imagination Library, a not-for-profit
program designed to inspire a love of reading and learning, sponsored in part by The
Dollywood Foundation. Penguin's trade editions of this work are available wherever
books are sold.

It was Brooklyn.

It was summer.

It was baseball.

All day long the kids on Bedford Avenue
played stickball in the streets.

Except for Luke.

"When you're older," his big brother, Nicky, told him.

"He's just a squirt," one of the other kids said, laughing.

So Luke watched the games from the curb, and then he'd practice.

He threw a ball against the wall next to the deli. He practiced his swing over and over again. He ran as fast as he could up and down the block.

He wanted to be ready when it was time.

And at night, whenever the
Dodgers were playing, Luke hurried
up to the roof, where he could see
the lights of Ebbets Field. When
he heard the crowd go wild, he
imagined his favorite player, Jackie
Robinson, had hit a home run.

Someday, Luke thought, I will
hit a home run, too.

Finally, one morning, the team was short a player.

"Franky had to go to his aunt's!"

"Who we gonna get?"

"Hey," said Luke, "what about me?"

Everyone was quiet.

"Aw, come on," said his brother. "Give him a chance."

"We got nobody else."

"He better not mess up."

They put him in left field. No balls came his way, so he just stood there.

When it was his turn up at bat, Luke took a few practice swings, then stepped up to the plate.

"I'll show them," Luke muttered.

The ball whizzed past.

"Strike one!"

Luke held the bat higher.

"Strike two!"

Luke was barely in position when the next ball flew past and the catcher yelled, "Out!"

"You stink," Luke heard.

He got up to bat one more time but struck out again.

"Sometimes it just goes that way," his brother told him.

Franky came back in the afternoon, so Luke spent the rest of the day on the curb. He was sure they'd never let him play again.

Grandma was in the kitchen when he got home.

"I finally got a chance to play with the team," Luke told her.

Grandma could tell that the game hadn't gone well. "Not everyone plays like Jackie Robinson all the time," she said. "Not even Jackie Robinson."

Luke didn't smile.

"By the way," Grandma said, "are you doing anything tomorrow night?"

Luke shrugged.

"Well, if you're so busy, someone else will have to go with me to the game at Ebbets Field."

"What? You mean a real game?"

Grandma held up two tickets.

Ebbets Field was ablaze with lights. But this time, Luke didn't have to imagine the game.

"Thanks for taking me, Grandma," he said.

They watched the Dodgers and Phillies battle it out. The game went into extra innings. By the time the Dodgers got up to bat in the bottom of the fourteenth inning, the score was still tied, 8–8. With two outs, Jackie Robinson was up.

The crowd roared.

"Come on, Jackie!" Luke yelled.

The pitcher threw a curveball.
Jackie swung.

"Strike one!" the umpire called.

The pitcher wound up. He threw
a fastball and Jackie missed.

"Strike two!"

Three balls followed.

All eyes at Ebbets Field rested on
Jackie. The Dodgers could still win.

Luke shouted with the crowd. "Give it to 'em, Jackie! You show 'em!"

Jackie looked around from under his cap, then dug his feet into the dirt.

The pitcher began his windup.

"You can do it, Jackie," Luke whispered. "You can do it."

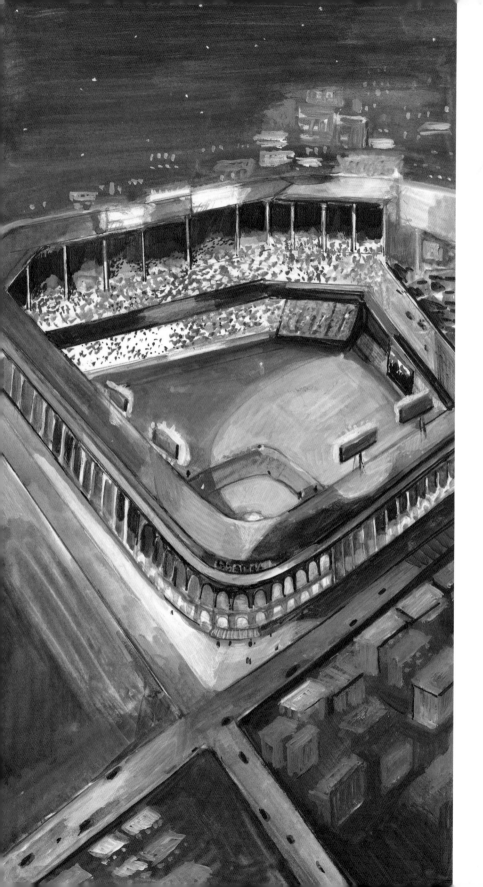

Suddenly, Luke heard the loud crack of a bat. When he looked up, the ball was flying over his head, flying over the scoreboard, flying over the walls of Ebbets Field! The crowd went wild!

Luke stood up on his seat and cheered, "You showed 'em, Jackie!"

"What a game!" Grandma said. "See, you can't give up. Even Jackie Robinson's got to keep trying."

Luke didn't answer.

When Luke got home, he ran up to the roof. The lights were going out at Ebbets Field.

"Come on down! It's bedtime!" Nicky called.

Just then, Luke saw a ball lying on the ground.

"Look!" he said, picking it up. "This is the home run ball that Jackie Robinson hit tonight!"

"Naw. That's just some old ball a kid hit up on the roof," Nick said, laughing, as he went downstairs.

And that's when Luke saw him.
It was Jackie Robinson himself.
"I hit that one for you, kid."
Before Luke could say a word,
Jackie ran to the dugout to join
the other Dodgers. But he looked
back one more time.

"Hey, kid," he said. "Your grandma was right. You can't give up."

"Thanks, Mr. Robinson."

The final lights went out at Ebbets Field. Luke looked down at the winning ball and smiled.

"I won't," he whispered to himself.

And he didn't.